THE RAILWAY STORIES
The Rev. W. Awdry

HENRY THE GREEN ENGINE

TOBY THE TRAM ENGINE

GORDON THE BIG ENGINE

WITH ILLUSTRATIONS BY

C. REGINALD DALBY

This edition first published in Great Britain in 1982 by
Octopus Books Limited
59 Grosvenor Street
London W1

Henry the Green Engine first published in Great Britain
in 1951 by Edmund Ward (Publishers) Ltd
Copyright © 1967 Kaye & Ward Ltd
Toby the Tram Engine first published in Great Britain
in 1952 by Edmund Ward (Publishers) Ltd
Copyright 1952 Edmund Ward (Publishers) Ltd
Copyright © 1970 Kaye & Ward Ltd
Gordon the Big Engine first published in Great Britain
in 1953 by Edmund Ward (Publishers) Ltd
Copyright © 1953 Edmund Ward (Publishers) Ltd
Copyright © 1970 Kaye & Ward Ltd

This arrangement © 1982 Octopus Books Limited

Fifth impression, reprinted 1984

ISBN 0 86273 054 6

Produced by
Mandarin Publishers Limited
22a Westlands Road
Quarry Bay, Hong Kong

Printed in Hong Kong

THE RAILWAY STORIES

CONTENTS

HENRY THE GREEN ENGINE

TOBY THE TRAM ENGINE

GORDON THE BIG ENGINE

HENRY THE GREEN ENGINE
COAL

"I suffer dreadfully, and no one cares."

"Rubbish, Henry," snorted James, "you don't work hard enough."

Henry was bigger than James, but smaller than Gordon. Sometimes he could pull trains; sometimes he had no strength at all.

The Fat Controller spoke to him too. "You are too expensive, Henry. You have had lots of new parts and new paint too, but they've done you no good. If we can't make you better, we must get another engine instead of you."

This made Henry, his Driver, and his Fireman very sad.

The Fat Controller was waiting when Henry came to the platform. He had taken off his hat and coat, and put on overalls.

He climbed to the footplate and Henry started.

"Henry is a 'bad steamer,'" said the Fireman. "I build up his fire, but it doesn't give enough heat."

Henry tried very hard, but it was no good. He had not enough steam, and they stopped outside Edward's station.

"Oh dear!" thought Henry sadly, "I shall have to go away."

Edward took charge of the train. Henry stopped behind.

"What do you think is wrong, Fireman?" asked the Fat Controller.

The Fireman mopped his face. "Excuse me, sir," he answered, "but the coal is wrong. We've had a poor lot lately, and today it's worse. The other engines can manage; they have big fireboxes. Henry's is small and can't make the heat. With Welsh coal he'd be a different engine."

"It's expensive," said the Fat Controller thoughtfully, "but Henry must have a fair chance. James shall go and fetch some."

When the Welsh coal came, Henry's Driver and Fireman were excited.

"Now we'll show them, Henry old fellow!" They carefully oiled all his joints and polished his brass till it shone like gold.

His fire had already been lit, so the Fireman "made it" carefully. He put large lumps of coal like a wall round the outside. Then he covered the glowing middle part with smaller lumps.

"You're spoiling my fire," complained Henry.

"Wait and see," said the Fireman. "We'll have a roaring fire just when we want it."

He was right. When Henry reached the platform, the water was boiling nicely, and he had to let off steam, to show how happy he was. He made such a noise that the Fat Controller came out to see him.

"How are you, Henry?"

"Pip peep peep!" whistled Henry, "I feel fine!"

"Have you a good fire, Driver?"

"Never better sir, *and* plenty of steam."

"No record breaking," warned the Fat Controller, smiling. "Don't push him too hard."

"Henry won't need pushing, sir; I'll have to hold him back."

Henry had a lovely day. He had never felt so well in his life. He wanted to go fast, but his Driver wouldn't let him. "Steady old fellow," he would say, "there's plenty of time."

They arrived early at the Junction.

"Where have you been, lazibones?" asked Henry, when Thomas puffed in, "I can't wait for dawdling Tank Engines like you! Good-bye!"

"Whoooosh!" said Thomas to Annie and Clarabel as Henry disappeared, "have you ever seen anything like it?"

Both Annie and Clarabel agreed that they never had.

THE FLYING KIPPER

Lots of ships use the harbour at the big station by the sea. The passenger ships have spotless paint and shining brass. Other ships, though smaller and dirtier, are important too. They take coal, machinery and other things abroad, and bring back meat, timber and things we need.

Fishing boats also come there. They unload their fish on the quay. Some of it is sent to shops in the town, and some goes in a special train to other places far away.

The railwaymen call this train "The Flying Kipper."

One winter evening Henry's Driver said: "We'll be out early tomorrow. We've got to take 'The Flying Kipper'."

"Don't tell Gordon," he whispered, "but I think if we pull the 'Kipper' nicely, the Fat Controller will let us pull the Express."

"Hurrah!" cried Henry, excited. "That will be lovely."

He was ready at 5 o'clock. There was snow and frost. Men hustled and shouted, loading the vans with crates of fish. The last door banged, the Guard showed his green lamp, and they were off.

"Come on! Come on! dontbesilly! — dontbesilly!" puffed Henry to the vans, as his wheels slipped on the icy rails.

The vans shuddered and groaned. "Trock, Trick, Trock, Trick; all right, all right," they answered grudgingly.

"That is better, that is better," puffed Henry more happily, as the train began to gather speed.

Thick clouds of smoke and steam poured from his funnel into the cold air; and when his Fireman put on more coal, the fire's light shone brightly on the snow around.

"Hurry, hurry, hurry," panted Henry.

They hooshed under bridges, and clattered through stations, green signal-lights showing as they passed.

They were going well, the light grew better and a yellow signal appeared ahead.

"Distant signal — up," thought Henry, "caution." His Driver, shutting off steam, prepared to stop, but the home signal was down. "All clear, Henry; away we go."

They couldn't know the points from the main line to a siding were frozen, and that that signal had been set at "danger." A fall of snow had forced it down.

A goods train waited in the siding to let "The Flying

Kipper" pass. The Driver and Fireman were drinking cocoa in the brake-van.

The Guard pulled out his watch. "The 'Kipper' is due," he said.

"Who cares?" said the Fireman. "This is good cocoa."

The Driver got up, "Come on Fireman, back to our engine."

"Hey!" the Fireman grumbled, "I haven't finished my cocoa yet."

A sudden crash – the brake-van broke – the three men shot in the air like Jacks-in-the-box, and landed in the snow outside.

Henry's Driver and Fireman jumped clear before the crash. The Fireman fell head first into a heap of snow. He kicked so hard that the Driver couldn't pull him out.

Henry sprawled on his side. He looked surprised. The goods train Fireman waved his empty mug.

"You clumsy great engine! The best cup of cocoa I've ever had, and you bump into me and spill it all!"

"Never mind your cocoa, Fireman," laughed his Driver, "run and telephone the breakdown gang."

The gang soon cleared the line, but they had hard work lifting Henry to the rails.

The Fat Controller came to see him.

"The signal was down, sir," said Henry nervously.

"Cheer up, Henry! It wasn't your fault. Ice and snow caused the accident. I'm sending you to Crewe, a fine place for sick engines. They'll give you a new shape and a larger firebox. Then you'll feel a different engine, and won't need special coal any more. Won't that be nice?"

"Yes, sir," said Henry doubtfully.

Henry liked being at Crewe, but was glad to come home.

A crowd of people waited to see him arrive in his new shape. He looked so splendid and strong that they gave him three cheers.

"Peep peep pippippeep! Thank you very much," he whistled happily.

I am sorry to say that a lot of little boys are often late for school because they wait to see Henry go by!

They often see him pulling the Express; and he does it so well that Gordon is jealous. But that is another story.

Gordon's Whistle

Gordon was cross.

"Why should Henry have a new shape?" he grumbled. "A shape good enough for ME is good enough for him. He goes gallivanting off to Crewe, leaving us to do his work. It's disgraceful!"

"And there's another thing. Henry whistles too much. No *respectable* engine ever whistles loudly at stations."

"It isn't wrong," said Gordon, "but we just don't do it."

Poor Henry didn't feel happy any more.

"Never mind," whispered Percy, "I'm glad you are home again; I like your whistling."

"Goodbye, Henry," called Gordon next morning as he left the shed. "We are glad to have you with us again, but be sure and remember what I said about whistling."

Later on Henry took a slow train, and presently stopped at Edward's station.

"Hullo Henry," said Edward, "you look splendid; I was pleased to hear your happy whistle yesterday."

"Thank you, Edward," smiled Henry ... "Sh Sh! Can you hear something?"

Edward listened – far away, but getting louder and louder, was the sound of an engine's whistle.

"It sounds like Gordon," said Edward, "and it ought to be Gordon, but Gordon never whistles like that."

It *was* Gordon.

He came rushing down the hill at a tremendous rate. He didn't look at Henry, and he didn't look at Edward; he was purple in the boiler, and whistling fit to burst.

He screamed through the station and disappeared.

"Well!!!" said Edward, looking at Henry.

"It isn't wrong," chuckled Henry, "but we just don't do it," and he told Edward what Gordon had said.

Meanwhile Gordon screeched along the line. People came out of their houses, air-raid sirens started, five fire brigades got ready to go out, horses upset their carts, and old ladies dropped their parcels.

At a big station the noise was awful. Porters and passengers held their ears. The Fat Controller held his ears too; he gave a lot of orders, but no one could hear them, and Gordon went on whistling. At last he clambered into Gordon's cab.

"Take him away," he bellowed, "AND STOP THAT NOISE!"

Still whistling, Gordon puffed sadly away.

He whistled as he crossed the points; he whistled on the siding; he was still whistling as the last deafened passenger left the station.

Then two fitters climbed up and knocked his whistle valve into place ——

—— and there was SILENCE.

Gordon slunk into the shed. He was glad it was empty.

The others came in later. "It isn't wrong," murmured Henry to no one in particular, "but we just don't do it."

No one mentioned whistles!

PERCY AND THE TROUSERS

On cold mornings Percy often saw workmen wearing scarves.

"My funnel's cold, my funnel's cold!" he would puff; "I want a scarf, I want a scarf."

"Rubbish, Percy," said Henry one day, "engines don't want scarves!"

"Engines with proper funnels do," said Percy in his cheeky way. "You've only got a small one!"

Henry snorted; he was proud of his short, neat funnel.

Just then a train came in and Percy, still puffing "I want a scarf, I want a scarf," went to take the coaches to their siding.

His Driver always shut off steam just outside the station, and Percy would try to surprise the coaches by coming in as quietly as he could.

Two porters were taking some luggage across the line. They had a big load and were walking backwards, to see that none fell off the trolley.

Percy arrived so quietly that the porters didn't hear him till the trolley was on the line. The porters jumped clear. The trolley disappeared with a crunch.

Boxes and bags burst in all directions.

"Oo——oohe——r!" groaned Percy and stopped. Sticky streams of red and yellow jam trickled down his face. A top-hat hung on his lamp-iron. Clothes, hats, boots, shoes, skirts and blouses stuck to his front. A pair of striped trousers coiled lovingly round his funnel. They were grey no longer!

Angry passengers looked at their broken trunks. The Fat Controller seized the top-hat.

"Mine!" he said crossly.

"Percy," he shouted, "look at this."

"Yes sir, I am sir," a muffled voice replied.

"My best trousers too!"

"Yes sir, please sir," said Percy nervously.

"I am very cross," said the Fat Controller. "We must pay the passengers for their spoilt clothes. My hat is dented, and my trousers are ruined, all because you *will* come into the station as if you were playing 'Grandmother's Steps' with the coaches."

The Driver unwound the trousers.

The Fat Controller waved them away.

"Percy wanted a scarf; he shall have my trousers for a scarf; they will keep him warm."

Percy wore them back to the yard.

He doesn't like scarves now!

This story is adapted from one told by Mr C. Hamilton Ellis in *The Trains We Loved*. We gratefully acknowledge his permission to use it.

HENRY'S SNEEZE

One lovely Saturday morning, Henry was puffing along.
The sun shone, the fields were green, the birds sang; Henry
had plenty of steam in his boiler, and he was feeling happy.

"I feel so well, I feel so well," he sang.

"Trickety trock, Trickety trock," hummed his coaches.

Henry saw some boys on a bridge.

"Peep! Peep! Hullo!" he whistled cheerfully.

"Peep! Peep! Peeeep!" he called the next moment. "Oh!
Oh! Oooh!" For the boys didn't wave and take his number;
they dropped stones on him instead.

They were silly, stupid boys who thought it would be fun to drop stones down his funnel. Some of the stones hit Henry's boiler and spoilt his paint; one hit the Fireman on the head as he was shovelling coal, and others broke the carriage windows.

"It's a shame, it's a shame," hissed Henry.

"They've broken our glass, they've broken our glass," sobbed the coaches.

The Driver opened the first-aid box, bandaged the Fireman's head, and planned what he was going to do.

They stopped the train and the Guard asked if any passengers were hurt. No one was hurt, but everyone was cross. They saw the Fireman's bumped head, and told him what to do for it, and they looked at Henry's paint.

"Call the Police," they shouted angrily.

"No!" said the Driver, "leave it to Henry and me. We'll teach those lads a lesson."

"What will you do?" they asked.

"Can you keep a secret?"

"Yes, yes," they all said.

"Well then," said the Driver, "Henry is going to sneeze at them."

"What!" cried all the passengers.

The Driver laughed. "Henry draws air in through his fire, and puffs it out with smoke and steam. When he puffs hard, the air blows ashes from his fire into his smoke box, and these ashes sometimes prevent him puffing properly.

"When your nose is blocked, you sometimes sneeze. If Henry's smoke box is blocked, I can make air and steam blow the ashes out through his funnel.

"We will do it at the bridge and startle those boys."

Henry puffed on to the terminus, where he had a rest. Then he took the train back. Lots of people were waiting at the station just before the bridge. They wanted to see what would happen.

"Henry has plenty of ashes," said the Driver. "Please keep all the windows shut till we have passed the bridge. Henry is as excited as we are, aren't you old fellow?" and he patted Henry's boiler.

Henry didn't answer; he was feeling "stuffed up," but he winked at his Driver, like this.

The Guard's flag waved, his whistle blew, and they were off. Soon in the distance they saw the bridge. There were the boys, and they all had stones.

"Are you ready, Henry?" said his Driver. "Sneeze hard when I tell you."

"NOW!" he said, and turned the handle.

"Atisha Atisha Atishoooooh!"

Smoke and steam and ashes spouted from his funnel. They went all over the bridge, and all over the boys who ran away as black as soot.

"Well done, Henry," laughed his Driver, "they won't drop stones on engines again."

"Your coat is all black, but we'll rub you down and paint your scratches and you'll be as good as new tomorrow."

Henry has never again sneezed under a bridge. The Fat Controller doesn't like it. His smoke box is always cleaned in the yard while he is resting.

He has now gone under more bridges than he can count; but from that day to this there have been no more boys with stones.

TOBY THE TRAM ENGINE

TOBY AND THE STOUT GENTLEMAN

Toby is a tram engine. He is short and sturdy. He has cow-catchers and side-plates, and doesn't look like a steam engine at all. He takes trucks from farms and factories to the main line, and the big engines take them to London and elsewhere. His tramline runs along roads and through fields and villages. Toby rings his bell cheerfully to everyone he meets.

He has a coach called Henrietta, who has seen better days. She complains because she has few passengers. Toby is attached to Henrietta and always takes her with him.

"She might be useful one day," he says.

"It's not fair at all!" grumbles Henrietta as the 'buses roar past full of passengers. She remembers that she used to be full, and nine trucks would rattle behind her.

Now there are only three or four, for the farms and factories send their goods mostly by lorry.

Toby is always careful on the road. The cars, 'buses and lorries often have accidents. Toby hasn't had an accident for years, but the 'buses are crowded, and Henrietta is empty.

"I can't understand it," says Toby the tram engine.

People come to see Toby, but they come by 'bus. They stare at him. "Isn't he quaint!" they say, and laugh.

They make him so cross.

One day a car stopped close by, and a little boy jumped out. "Come on Bridget," he called to his sister, and together they ran across to Toby. Two ladies and a stout gentleman followed. The gentleman looked important, but nice.

The children ran back. "Come on grandfather, do look at this engine," and seizing his hands they almost dragged him along.

"That's a tram engine, Stephen," said the stout gentleman.

"Is it electric?" asked Bridget.

"Whoosh!" hissed Toby crossly.

"Sh Sh!" said her brother, "you've offended him."

"But trams *are* electric, aren't they?"

"They are mostly," the stout gentleman answered, "but this is a steam tram."

"May we go in it grandfather? Please!"

The Guard had begun to blow his whistle.

"Stop," said the stout gentleman, and raised his hand. The Guard, surprised, opened his mouth, and the whistle fell out.

While he was picking it up, they all scrambled into Henrietta.

"Hip Hip Hurray!" chanted Henrietta, and she rattled happily behind.

Toby did not sing. "Electric indeed! Electric indeed," he snorted. He was very hurt.

The stout gentleman and his family got out at the junction, but waited for Toby to take them back to their car.

"What is your name?" asked the stout gentleman.

"Toby, Sir."

"Thank you, Toby, for a very nice ride."

"Thank *you*, Sir," said Toby politely. He felt better now.

"This gentleman," he thought, "is a gentleman who knows how to speak to engines."

The children came every day for a fortnight. Sometimes they rode with the Guard, sometimes in empty trucks, and on the last day of all the Driver invited them into his cab.

All were sorry when they had to go away.

Stephen and Bridget said "Thank you" to Toby, his Driver, his Fireman, and the Guard.

The stout gentleman gave them all a present.

"Peep pip pip peep," whistled Toby. "Come again soon."

"We will, we will," called the children, and they waved till Toby was out of sight.

The months passed. Toby had few trucks, and fewer passengers.

"Our last day, Toby," said his Driver sadly one morning. "The Manager says we must close tomorrow."

That day Henrietta had more passengers than she could manage. They rode in the trucks and crowded in the brake-van, and the Guard hadn't enough tickets to go round.

The passengers joked and sang, but Toby and his Driver wished they wouldn't.

"Goodbye, Toby," said the passengers afterwards, "we are sorry your line is closing down."

"So am I," said Toby sadly.

The last passenger left the station, and Toby puffed slowly to his shed.

"Nobody wants me," he thought, and went unhappily to sleep.

Next morning the shed was flung open, and he woke with a start to see his Fireman dancing a jig outside. His Driver, excited, waved a piece of paper.

"Wake up, Toby," they shouted, "and listen to this; it's a letter from the stout gentleman."

Toby listened and . . . .

But I mustn't tell you any more, or I should spoil the next story.

THOMAS IN TROUBLE

There is a line to a quarry at the end of Thomas's Branch; it goes for some distance along the road.

Thomas was always very careful here in case anyone was coming.

"Peep pip peep!" he whistled; then the people got out of the way, and he puffed slowly along, with his trucks rumbling behind him.

Early one morning there was no one on the road, but a large policeman was sitting on the grass close to the line. He was shaking a stone from his boot.

Thomas liked policemen. He had been a great friend of the Constable who used to live in the village; but he had just retired.

Thomas expected that the new Constable would be friendly too.

"Peep peep," he whistled, "good morning."

The policeman jumped and dropped his boot. He scrambled up, and hopped round on one leg till he was facing Thomas.

Thomas was sorry to see that he didn't look friendly at all. He was red in the face and very cross.

The policeman wobbled about, trying to keep his balance.

"Disgraceful!" he spluttered. "I didn't sleep a wink last night, it was so quiet, and now engines come whistling suddenly behind me! My first day in the country too!"

He picked up his boot and hopped over to Thomas.

"I'm sorry, Sir," said Thomas, "I only said 'good morning'."

The policeman grunted, and, leaning against Thomas's buffer, he put his boot on.

He drew himself up and pointed to Thomas.

"Where's your cow-catcher?" he asked accusingly.

"But I don't catch cows, Sir!"

"Don't be funny!" snapped the policeman. He looked at Thomas's wheels. "No side plates either," and he wrote in his notebook.

"Engines going on Public Roads must have their wheels covered, and a cow-catcher in front. You haven't, so you are Dangerous to the Public."

"Rubbish!" said his Driver, "we've been along here hundreds of times and never had an accident."

"That makes it worse," the policeman answered. He wrote "regular law breaker" in his book.

Thomas puffed sadly away.

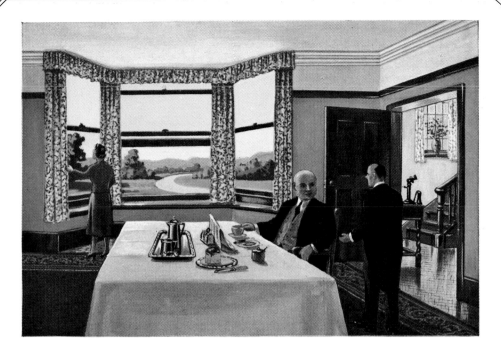

The Fat Controller was having breakfast. He was eating toast and marmalade. He had the newspaper open in front of him, and his wife had just given him some more coffee.

The butler knocked and came in.

"Excuse me, Sir, you are wanted on the telephone."

"Bother that telephone!" said the Fat Controller.

"I'm sorry, my dear," he said a few minutes later, "Thomas is in trouble with the police, and I must go at once."

He gulped down his coffee and hurried from the room.

At the junction, Thomas's Driver told the Fat Controller what had happened.

"Dangerous to the Public indeed; we'll see about that!" and he climbed grimly into Annie the coach.

The policeman was on the platform at the other end. The Fat Controller spoke to him at once, and a crowd collected to listen.

Other policemen came to see what was happening and the Fat Controller argued with them too; but it was no good.

"The Law is the Law," they said, "and we can't change it."

The Fat Controller felt exhausted.

He mopped his face.

"I'm sorry Driver," he said, "it's no use arguing with policemen. We will have to make those cow-catcher things for Thomas, I suppose."

"Everyone will laugh, Sir," said Thomas sadly, "they'll say I look like a Tram."

The Fat Controller stared, then he laughed.

"Well done, Thomas! Why didn't I think of it before? We want a Tram Engine! When I was on my holiday, I met a nice little engine called Toby. He hasn't enough work to do, and needs a change. I'll write to his Controller at once."

A few days later Toby arrived.

"That's a good engine," said the Fat Controller, "I see you've brought Henrietta."

"You don't mind, do you, Sir?" asked Toby anxiously. "The Station Master wanted to use her as a hen house, and that would never do."

"No, indeed," said the Fat Controller gravely, "we couldn't allow that."

Toby made the trucks behave even better than Thomas did.

At first Thomas was jealous, but he was so pleased when Toby rang his bell and made the policeman jump that they have been firm friends ever since.

DIRTY OBJECTS

Toby and Henrietta take the workmen to the quarry every morning. At the junction they often meet James.

Toby and Henrietta were shabby when they first came, and needed new paint. James was very rude. "Ugh! What *dirty* objects!" he would say.

At last Toby lost patience.

"James," he asked, "why are you red?"

"I am a splendid engine," answered James loftily, "ready for anything. You never see *my* paint dirty."

"Oh!" said Toby innocently, "that's why you once needed

boot-laces; to be ready, I suppose."

James went redder than ever, and snorted off.

At the end of the line James left his coaches and got ready for his next train. It was a "slow goods", stopping at every station to pick up and set down trucks. James hated slow goods trains.

"Dirty trucks from dirty sidings! Ugh!" he grumbled.

Starting with only a few, he picked up more and more trucks at each station, till he had a long train. At first the trucks behaved well, but James bumped them so crossly that they determined to pay him out.

Presently, rumbling over the viaduct, they approached the top of Gordon's hill. Heavy goods trains halt here to "pin down" their brakes. James had had an accident with trucks before, and should have remembered this.

"Wait, James, wait," said his Driver, but James wouldn't wait. He was too busy thinking what he would say to Toby when they next met.

Too late he saw where he was, and tried to stop.

"Hurrah! Hurrah!" laughed the trucks, and banging their buffers they pushed him down the hill.

The Guard tightened his brakes until they screamed.

"On! on! on!" yelled the trucks.

"I've *got* to stop, I've *got* to stop," groaned James, and setting his brakes he managed to check the truck's mad rush, but they were still going much too fast to stop in time.

Through the station they thundered, and lurched into the yard.

James shut his eyes ———

There was a bursting crash, and something sticky splashed all over him. He had run into two tar wagons, and was black from smokebox to cab.

James was more dirty than hurt, but the tar wagons and

some of the trucks were all to pieces. The Breakdown-train was in the yard, and they soon tidied up the mess.

Toby and Percy were sent to help, and came as quickly as they could.

"Look here, Percy!" exclaimed Toby, "whatever is that dirty object?"

"That's James; didn't you know?"

"It's James's shape," said Toby thoughtfully, "but James is a splendid red engine, and you never see *his* paint dirty."

James shut his eyes, and pretended he hadn't heard.

They cleared away the unhurt trucks, and helped James home.

The Fat Controller met them.

"Well done, Percy and Toby," he said.

He turned to James. "Fancy letting your trucks run away. I *am* surprised. You're not fit to be seen; you must be cleaned at once."

"Toby shall have a coat of paint ———— chocolate and blue I think."

"Please, Sir, can Henrietta have one too?"

"Certainly Toby," he smiled, "she shall have brown like Annie and Clarabel."

"Oh thank you, Sir! She will be pleased."

Toby ran home happily to tell her the news.

MRS KYNDLEY'S CHRISTMAS

It was nearly Christmas. Annie and Clarabel were packed full of people and parcels.

Thomas was having very hard work.

"Come on! Come on!" he puffed.

"We're feeling *so* full!" grumbled the coaches.

Thomas looked at the hill ahead. "Can I do it? Can I do it?" he puffed anxiously.

Suddenly he saw a handkerchief waving from a cottage window. He felt better at once.

"Yes I can, yes I can," he puffed bravely. He pulled his

hardest, and was soon through the tunnel and resting in the Station.

"That was Mrs Kyndley who waved to you, Thomas," his Driver told him. "She has to stay in bed all day."

"Poor lady," said Thomas, "I am sorry for her."

Engines have heavy loads at Christmas time, but Thomas and Toby didn't mind the hard work when they saw Mrs Kyndley waving.

But then it began to rain. It rained for days and days.

Thomas didn't like it, nor did his Driver.

"Off we go Thomas!" he would say. "Pull hard and get home quickly; Mrs Kyndley won't wave today."

But whether she waved or not, they always whistled when they passed the little lonely cottage. Its white walls stood out against the dark background of the hills.

"Hello!" exclaimed Thomas's Fireman one day. "Look at that!"

The Driver came across the cab. "Something's wrong there," he said.

Hanging flapping and bedraggled from a window of the cottage was something that looked like a large red flag.

"Mrs Kyndley needs help I expect," said the Driver, and put on the brakes. Thomas gently stopped.

The Guard came squelching through the rain up to Thomas's cab, and the Driver pointed to the flag.

"See if a Doctor's on the train and ask him to go to the cottage; then walk back to the station and tell them we've stopped."

The Fireman went to see if the line was clear in front.

Two passengers left the train and climbed to the cottage. Then the Fireman returned.

"We'll back down to the station," said the Driver, "so that Thomas can get a good start."

"We shan't get up the hill," the Fireman answered. "Come and see what's happened!"

They walked along the line round the bend.

"Jiminy Christmas!" exclaimed the Driver, "go back to the train; I'm going to the cottage."

He found the Doctor with Mrs Kyndley.

"Silly of me to faint," she said.

"You saw the red dressing-gown? You're all safe?" asked Mrs Kyndley.

"Yes," smiled the Driver, "I've come to thank you. There was a landslide in the cutting, Doctor, and Mrs Kyndley saw it from her window and stopped us. She's saved our lives!"

"God bless you, ma'am," said the Driver, and tiptoed from the room.

They cleared the line by Christmas Day, and the sun shone as a special train puffed up from the junction.

First came Toby, then Thomas with Annie and Clarabel, and last of all, but very pleased at being allowed to come, was Henrietta.

The Fat Controller was there, and lots of other people who wanted to say "Thank you" to Mrs Kyndley.

"Peepeep, Peepeep! Happy Christmas!" whistled the engines as they reached the place.

The people got out and climbed to the cottage. Thomas and Toby wished they could go too.

Mrs Kyndley's husband met them at the door.

The Fat Controller, Thomas's Driver, Fireman, and Guard went upstairs, while the others stood in the sunshine below the window.

The Driver gave her a new dressing-gown to replace the one spoilt by the rain. The Guard brought her some grapes, and the Fireman gave her some woolly slippers, and promised to bring some coal as a present from Thomas, next time they passed.

Mrs Kyndley was very pleased with her presents.

"You are very good to me," she said.

"The passengers and I," said the Fat Controller, "hope you will accept these tickets for the South Coast, Mrs Kyndley, and get really well in the sunshine. We cannot thank you enough for preventing that accident. I hope we have not tired you. Goodbye and a happy Christmas."

Then going quietly downstairs, they joined the group outside the window, and sang some carols before returning to the train.

Mrs Kyndley is now at Bournemouth, getting better every day, and Thomas and Toby are looking forward to the time when they can welcome her home.

GORDON THE BIG ENGINE

OFF THE RAILS

Gordon was resting in a siding.

"Peep peep! Peep peep! Hullo, Fatface!" whistled Henry.

"What cheek!" spluttered Gordon. "That Henry is too big for his wheels; fancy speaking to me like that! Me e e e!" he went on, letting off steam, "Me e e e who has never had an accident!"

"Aren't jammed whistles and burst safety valves accidents?" asked Percy innocently.

"No indeed!" said Gordon huffily, "high spirits – might happen to any engine; but to come off the rails, well I ask you! Is it right? Is it decent?"

A few days later it was Henry's turn to take the Express. Gordon watched him getting ready.

"Be careful, Henry," he said, "you're not pulling the 'Flying Kipper' now; mind you keep on the rails today."

Henry snorted away, Gordon yawned and went to sleep.

But he didn't sleep long. "Wake up, Gordon," said his Driver, "a Special train's coming and we're to pull it."

Gordon opened his eyes. "Is it Coaches or Trucks?"

"Trucks," said his Driver.

"Trucks!" said Gordon crossly. "Pah!"

They lit Gordon's fire and oiled him ready for the run. The fire was sulky and wouldn't burn; but they couldn't wait, so Edward pushed him to the Turn-table to get him facing the right way.

"I *won't* go, I *won't* go," grumbled Gordon.

"Don't be silly, don't be silly," puffed Edward.

Gordon tried hard, but he couldn't stop himself being moved.

At last he was on the Turn-table, Edward was uncoupled and backed away, and Gordon's Driver and Fireman jumped down to turn him round.

The movement had shaken Gordon's fire; it was now burning nicely and making steam.

Gordon was cross, and didn't care what he did.

He waited till the Table was half-way round. "I'll show them! I'll show them!" he hissed, and moved slowly forward.

He only meant to go a little way, just far enough to "jam" the Table, and stop it turning, as he had done once before. But he couldn't stop himself, and, slithering down the embankment, he settled in a ditch.

"Oooosh!" he hissed as his wheels churned the mud. "Get me out! Get me out!"

"Not a hope," said his Driver and Fireman, "you're stuck, you silly great engine, don't you understand that?"

They telephoned the Fat Controller.

* * *

"So Gordon didn't want to take the Special and ran into a ditch," he answered from his office. "What's that you say? The Special's waiting – tell Edward to take it please – and Gordon? Oh leave him where he is; we haven't time to bother with him now."

A family of toads croaked crossly at Gordon as he lay in

the mud. On the other side of the ditch some little boys were chattering.

"Coo! Doesn't he look silly!"

"They'll never get him out."

They began to sing:

> Silly old Gordon fell in a ditch,
> fell in a ditch,
> fell in a ditch,
> Silly old Gordon fell in a ditch,
> All on a Monday morning.

The School bell rang and, still singing, they chased down the road.

"Pshaw!" said Gordon, and blew away three tadpoles and an inquisitive newt.

Gordon lay in the ditch all day.

"Oh dear!" he thought, "I shall never get out."

But that evening they brought floodlights; then with powerful jacks they lifted Gordon and made a road of sleepers under his wheels to keep him from the mud.

Strong wire ropes were fastened to his back end, and James and Henry, pulling hard, at last managed to bring him to the rails.

Late that night Gordon crawled home a sadder and a wiser engine!

LEAVES

Two men were cleaning Gordon.

"Mind my eye," Gordon grumbled.

"Shut it, silly! Did you ever see such mud, Bert?"

"No I never, Alf! You ought to be ashamed, Gordon, giving us extra work."

The hosing and scrubbing stopped. Gordon opened one eye, but shut it quickly.

"Wake up, Gordon," said the Fat Controller sternly, "and listen to me. You will pull no more coaches till you are a Really Useful Engine."

So Gordon had to spend his time pulling trucks.

"Goods trains, Goods trains," he muttered. He felt his position deeply.

"That's for you! – and *you*! – *and* you!" Gordon said crossly.

"Oh! Oh! Oh! Oh!" screamed the trucks as he shunted them about the yard.

"Trucks will be trucks," said James, watching him.

"They won't with *me*!" snorted Gordon. "I'll teach them. Go on!" and another truck scurried away.

"They tried to push me down the hill this morning," Gordon explained. "It's slippery there. You'll probably need some help."

"*I* don't need help on hills," said James huffily.

Gordon laughed, and got ready for his next train.

James went away to take the Express.

"Slippery hills indeed," he snorted. "*I* don't need help."

"Come on! Come on!" he puffed.

"All in good time, all in good time," grumbled the coaches.

The train was soon running nicely, but a "Distant" signal checked them close to Gordon's Hill.

Gordon's Hill used to be bleak and bare. Strong winds from the sea made it hard to climb. Trees were planted to give shelter, and in summer the trains run through a leafy avenue.

Now Autumn had come, and dead leaves fell. The wind usually puffed them away, but today rain made them heavy, and they did not move.

The "Home" signal showed "clear", and James began to go faster.

He started to climb the hill.

"I'll do it! I'll do it!" he puffed confidently.

Half-way up he was not so sure! "I *must* do it, I *must* do it," he panted desperately, but try as he would, his wheels slipped on the leaves, and he couldn't pull the train at all.

"Whatsthematter? Whatsthematter?" he gasped.

"Steady old boy, steady," soothed his Driver.

His Fireman put sand on the rails to help him grip; but James's wheels spun so fast that they only ground the sand and leaves to slippery mud, making things worse than before.

The train slowly stopped. Then —

"Help! Help! Help!" whistled James; for though his wheels were turning forwards, the heavy coaches pulled him backwards, and the whole train started slipping down the hill.

His Driver shut off steam, carefully put on the brakes, and skilfully stopped the train.

"Whew!" he sat down and mopped his face. "I've never known *that* happen before."

"I have," said the Fireman, "in Bincombe tunnel – Southern Region."

The Guard poked his head in the cab. "Now what?" he asked.

"Back to the station," said the Fireman, taking charge, "and send for a 'Banker'."

So the Guard warned the Signalman, and they brought the train safely down.

But Gordon, who had followed with a Goods train, saw what had happened.

Gordon left his trucks, and crossed over to James.

"I thought you could climb hills," he chuckled.

James didn't answer; he had no steam!

"Ah well! We live and learn," said Gordon, "we live and learn. Never mind, little James," he went on kindly, "I'm going to push behind. Whistle when you're ready."

James waited till he had plenty of steam, then "Peep! Peep!" he called.

"Poop! Poop! Poop!"

"Pull hard," puffed Gordon.

"We'll do it!" puffed James.

"Pull hard! We'll do it," the engines puffed together.

Clouds of smoke and steam towered from the snorting engines as they struggled up the hill.

"We *can* do it!" puffed James.

"We *will* do it!" puffed Gordon.

The greasy rails sometimes made Gordon's wheels slip, but he never gave up, and presently they reached the top.

"We've done it! We've done it!" they puffed.

Gordon stopped. "Poop! Poop!" he whistled. "Goodbye."

"Peep! Peep! Peep! Peep! Thank you! Goodbye," answered James. Gordon watched the coaches wistfully till they were out of sight; then slowly he trundled back to his waiting trucks.

DOWN THE MINE

One day Thomas was at the junction, when Gordon shuffled in with some trucks.

"Poof!" remarked Thomas, "what a funny smell!"

"Can you smell a smell?"

"I can't smell a smell," said Annie and Clarabel.

"A funny, musty sort of smell," said Thomas.

"No one noticed it till you did," grunted Gordon. "It must be yours."

"Annie! Clarabel! Do you know what I think it is?" whispered Thomas loudly. "It's ditchwater!"

Gordon snorted, but before he could answer, Thomas puffed quickly away.

Annie and Clarabel could hardly believe their ears!

"He's *dreadfully* rude; I feel quite ashamed." "I feel *quite* ashamed, he's dreadfully rude," they twittered to each other.

"You mustn't be rude, you make us ashamed," they kept telling Thomas.

But Thomas didn't care a bit.

"That was funny, that was funny," he chuckled. He felt very pleased with himself.

Annie and Clarabel were deeply shocked. They had a great respect for Gordon the Big Engine.

Thomas left the coaches at a station and went to a mine for some trucks.

Long ago, Miners, digging for lead, had made tunnels under the ground.

Though strong enough to hold up trucks, their roofs could not bear the weight of engines.

A large notice said: "DANGER. ENGINES MUST NOT PASS THIS BOARD."

Thomas had often been warned, but he didn't care.

"Silly old board," he thought. He had often tried to pass it, but had never succeeded.

This morning he laughed as he puffed along. He had

made a plan.

He had to push empty trucks into one siding, and pull out full ones from another.

His Driver stopped him, and the Fireman went to turn the points.

"Come on," waved the Fireman, and they started.

The Driver leaned out of the cab to see where they were going.

"Now!" said Thomas to himself, and, bumping the trucks fiercely, he jerked his Driver off the footplate.

"Hurrah!" laughed Thomas, and he followed the trucks into the siding.

"Stupid old board!" said Thomas as he passed it. "There's no danger; there's no danger."

His Driver, unhurt, jumped up. "Look out!" he shouted.

The Fireman clambered into the cab. Thomas squealed crossly as his brakes were applied.

"It's quite safe," he hissed.

"Come back," yelled the Driver, but before they could move, there was a rumbling and the rails quivered.

The Fireman jumped clear. As he did so the ballast slipped away and the rails sagged and broke.

"Fire and Smoke!" said Thomas, "I'm sunk!" – and he was!

Thomas could just see out of the hole, but he couldn't move.

"Oh dear!" he said, "I am a silly engine."

"And a very naughty one too," said a voice behind him, "I saw you."

"Please get me out; I won't be naughty again."

"I'm not so sure," replied the Fat Controller. "We can't lift you out with a crane, the ground's not firm enough. Hm . . . Let me see . . . I wonder if Gordon could pull you out."

"Yes Sir," said Thomas nervously. He didn't want to meet Gordon just yet!

"Down a mine is he? Ho! Ho! Ho!" laughed Gordon.

"What a joke! What a joke!" he chortled, puffing to the rescue.

"Poop! Poop! little Thomas," he whistled, "we'll have you out in a couple of puffs."

Strong cables were fastened between the two engines.

"Poop! Poop! Poop!"

"Are you ready? HEAVE," called the Fat Controller.

But they didn't pull Thomas out in two puffs; Gordon was panting hard and nearly purple before he had dragged Thomas out of the hole, and safely past the board.

"I'm sorry I was cheeky," said Thomas.

"That's all right, Thomas. You made me laugh. I like

that. I'm in disgrace," Gordon went on pathetically, "I feel very low."

"I'm in disgrace too," said Thomas.

"Why! so you are Thomas; we're both in disgrace. Shall we form an Alliance?"

"An Ally – what – was – it?"

"An Alliance, Thomas, 'United we stand, together we fall,'" said Gordon grandly.

"You help me, and I help you. How about it?"

"Right you are," said Thomas.

"Good! That's settled," rumbled Gordon.

And buffer to buffer the Allies puffed home.

Paint Pots and Queens

The stations on the Line were being painted.

The Engines were surprised.

"The Queen is coming," said the painters. The Engines in their shed were excited and wondered who would pull the Royal Train.

"I'm too old to pull important trains," said Edward sadly.

"I'm in disgrace," Gordon said gloomily. "The Fat Controller would never choose me."

"He'll choose me, of course," boasted James the Red Engine.

"You!" Henry snorted, "*You* can't climb hills. He will ask *me* to pull it, *and* I'll have a new coat of paint. You wait and see."

The days passed. Henry puffed about proudly, quite sure that he would be the Royal Engine.

One day when it rained, his Driver and Fireman stretched a tarpaulin from the cab to the tender, to keep themselves dry.

Henry puffed into the big station. A painter was climbing a ladder above the line. Henry's smoke puffed upwards; it was thick and black. The painter choked and couldn't see. He missed his footing on the ladder, dropped his paint pot, and fell plop on to Henry's tarpaulin.

The paint poured over Henry's boiler, and trickled down each side. The paint pot perched on his dome.

The painter clambered down and shook his brush at Henry.

"You spoil my clean paint with your dirty smoke," he said, "and then you take the whole lot, and make me go and fetch some more." He stumped crossly away.

The Fat Controller pushed through the crowd.

"You look like an iced cake, Henry," he said. "*That* won't do for the Royal Train. I must make other arrangements."

He walked over to the Yard.

Gordon and Thomas saw him coming, and both began to speak.

"Please Sir ————."

"One at a time," smiled the Fat Controller. "Yes Gordon?"

"May Thomas have his Branch Line again?"

"Hm," said the Fat Controller, "well Thomas?"

"Please, Sir, can Gordon pull coaches now?"

The Fat Controller pondered.

'Hm ———— you've both been quite good lately, and you deserve a treat ———— When the Queen comes, Edward will go in front and clear the line, Thomas will look after the coaches, and Gordon ———— will pull the train."

"Ooooh Sir!" said the engines happily.

The great day came. Percy, Toby, Henry and James worked hard bringing people to the Town.

Thomas sorted all their coaches in the Yard.

"Peep! Peep! Peep! They're coming!" Edward steamed in, looking smart with flags and bright paint.

Two minutes passed – five – seven – ten. "Poop! Poop!" Everyone knew that whistle, and a mighty cheer went up as the Queen's train glided into the Station.

Gordon was spotless, and his brass shone. Like Edward, he was decorated with flags, but on his buffer beam he proudly carried the Royal Arms.

The Queen was met by the Fat Controller, and before doing anything else, she thanked him for their splendid run.

"Not at all, Your Majesty," he said, "thank *you*."

"We have read," said the Queen to the Fat Controller, "a great deal about your engines. May we see them please?"

So he led the way to where all the engines were waiting.

"Peep! Peep!" whistled Toby and Percy, "they're coming!"

"Sh Sh! Sh Sh!" hissed Henry and James.

But Toby and Percy were too excited to care.

The Fat Controller told the Queen their names, and she talked to each engine. Then she turned to go.

Percy bubbled over, "Three cheers for the Queen!" he called.

"Peeeep! Peeeep! Peeeep!" whistled all the engines.

The Fat Controller held his ears, but the Queen, smiling, waved to the engines till she passed the gate.

Next day the Queen spoke specially to Thomas, who fetched her coaches, and to Edward and Gordon who took her away; and no engines ever felt prouder than Thomas, and Edward, and Gordon the **Big Engine**.

THE END